Dear Parent:
Your child's love of reading starts here!

Every child learns to read in a different way and at his or her own speed. Some go back and forth between reading levels and read favorite books again and again. Others read through each level in order. You can help your young reader improve and become more confident by encouraging his or her own interests and abilities. From books your child reads with you to the first books he or she reads alone, there are I Can Read Books for every stage of reading:

SHARED READING
Basic language, word repetition, and whimsical illustrations, ideal for sharing with your emergent reader

BEGINNING READING
Short sentences, familiar words, and simple concepts for children eager to read on their own

READING WITH HELP
Engaging stories, longer sentences, and language play for developing readers

READING ALONE
Complex plots, challenging vocabulary, and high-interest topics for the independent reader

ADVANCED READING
Short paragraphs, chapters, and exciting themes for the perfect bridge to chapter books

I Can Read Books have introduced children to the joy of reading since 1957. Featuring award-winning authors and illustrators and a fabulous cast of beloved characters, I Can Read Books set the standard for beginning readers.

A lifetime of discovery begins with the magical words **"I Can Read!"**

Visit www.icanread.com for information
on enriching your child's reading experience.

I Can Read Book® is a trademark of HarperCollins Publishers.

The Angry Birds™ Movie: Meet the Angry Birds
Based on the screenplay written by Jon Vitti

Library of Congress Control Number: 2015954423
ISBN 978-0-06-245332-7

Book design by Victor Joseph Ochoa

16 17 18 19 20 PC/WOR 10 9 8 7 6 5 4 3 ❖ First Edition

I Can Read!™

READING 2 WITH HELP

THE ANGRY BIRDS™ MOVIE

MEET THE ANGRY BIRDS

Adapted by Chris Cerasi

HARPER

An Imprint of HarperCollinsPublishers

Hi. My name is Red.

I am an Angry Bird.

My temper gets me into trouble.

I am the angriest bird around.

Most birds on Bird Island

are very happy.

Bird Island is a great place.

I live in a hut on the beach.

I love the peace and quiet.

I like being left alone.

Recently a family of blue birds

took me to bird court

because of my temper.

At bird court,

the judge settles disagreements.

He decided I was wrong.

"You *must* take

anger-management classes,"

said the judge.

I went to class.

I did not want to go inside.

The place looked too cheery.

I did not want to meet new birds.

I wanted to stay angry.

Matilda taught all the classes.

She used to be an Angry Bird.

Painting and yoga helped her relax.

She would teach us to relax, too.

Matilda was far too chirpy.

She really ruffled my feathers.

14

Matilda had the class
sit in a circle and talk.
I did not want to talk.
I did not want to listen
to other birds.

Chuck was the fastest bird

on Bird Island.

He walked fast.

He talked fast.

Chuck even slept fast!

His extra energy got him

into trouble.

Bomb was a big black bird

with a big problem.

He exploded

when he was happy or sad.

He exploded

when he was stressed or scared.

Bomb exploded *all the time*.
Bomb's hut was scorched
from too many explosions.
His explosions got him
into trouble.

Terence was the biggest bird.

Terence did not talk.

He growled.

We were too afraid to ask

what got him into trouble.

"Paint your anger," said Matilda.

Terence painted himself.

Bomb used lots of colors.

He made a big mess.

Chuck's painting looked like
a crazy maze.

Matilda asked me

to take the paintbrush.

I refused.

I did not want

to paint my anger.

Painting was not for me.

Matilda made us
try yoga poses.

Terrence just huffed
and puffed.
Bomb bent his arm
and lifted his leg.
He started to sweat.

Terence grunted and grumbled.

He tried so hard

to hold the poses.

I was good at one pose:

holding my head.

I needed the class to end.

I got my wish.

Someone grunted loudly.

It wasn't Terence.

It was Bomb.

He tilted to the left.

He tilted to the right.

He started shaking.

Then Bomb went *BOOM*!

Class was dismissed.

So I headed to
my favorite place:
home.